Jake Drake

TEACHER'S PET

Andrew Clements

illustrated by Dolores Avendaño

ALADDIN PAPERBACKS

New York   London   Toronto   Sydney   Singapore

P9-CRG-780

For Priscilla Avery,
the best neighbor a first-year teacher ever had
—A. C.

First Aladdin Paperbacks edition November 2001

ALADDIN PAPERBACKS
An imprint of Simon & Schuster Children's Publishing Division
1230 Avenue of the Americas
New York, NY 10020

Also available in a Simon & Schuster Books for Young Readers hardcover edition.

Designed by Lisa Vega
The text of this book was set in ITC Century Book.
The illustrations were done in pen and ink.

Manufactured in the United States of America

8 10 9 7

Library of Congress Control Number 2001053938
ISBN-13: 978-0-689-83882-8
ISBN-10: 0-689-83882-4

145133

Contents

CHAPTER ONE

FOUR BAD DAYS

I'm Jake—Jake Drake. I'm right in the middle of fourth grade. One thing I like about fourth grade is that I'm not in kindergarten, first grade, second grade, or third grade anymore. And I'm not at Miss Lulu's Dainty Diaper Day Care anymore either.

I think fourth grade is my best grade so far. It's so good that I have to think hard to remember anything about it that's bad at all. Like right now? I can only think of one day that wasn't so great. That was the day I thought my teacher Mr. Thompson was being unfair.

It was because of the way he treated Shawn

Underwood that day. First of all, Mr. Thompson picked Shawn to lead the Pledge of Allegiance. Then Mr. Thompson let Shawn take the attendance sheets to the office. During math, Mr. Thompson asked Shawn to write the answers on the chalkboard. After morning recess, Mr. Thompson let Shawn pick out the new chapter book for class read-aloud time. And then Mr. Thompson picked Shawn to line up first for lunch.

I know it sounds like I'm making too big a deal out of these things. But it was like Shawn was Mr. Thompson's favorite. It was like Shawn was the teacher's pet. And that's not fair.

Turns out I was wrong about Shawn, though. After lunch that day, Mr. Thompson said, "I have some good news, and some bad news. The good news is that at the end of the day we're going to have a party with cake and ice cream. But the bad news is that it's a going-away party for Shawn. Tomorrow Shawn is moving to another state, and we're all going to miss him a lot."

Mr. Thompson was being extra nice to Shawn because it was his last day. So Shawn wasn't really the teacher's pet. And I was glad because I liked Shawn, and being the teacher's pet is one of the worst things that can happen to a kid at school.

You know what stinks about being a teacher's pet? Everything, that's what.

I know this for sure because of what happened last May, right near the end of third grade. It all happened in four days—less than a week. But to me, those four days felt like four years. Because for those four days, I was in great danger.

I was in danger of losing my friends. I was in danger of losing my reputation. I was in danger of losing . . . my mind.

Because that was the time I became Jake Drake, Teacher's Pet.

When I was in third grade, we got five new computers in our classroom. Mrs. Snavin was my third-grade teacher, and she acted like computers were scary, especially the new ones. She always needed to look at a how-to book and the computer at the same time. Even then, she got mixed up a lot. Then she had to call Mrs. Reed, the librarian, to come and show her what to do.

So it was a Monday morning in May, and Mrs. Snavin was sitting in front of a new computer at the back of the room. She was confused about a program we were supposed to use for a math project. My desk was near the computers, and I was watching her.

Mrs. Snavin looked at the screen, and then she looked at this book, and then back at the screen again. Then she shook her head and let out this big sigh. I could tell she was almost ready to call Mrs. Reed.

I've always liked computers, and I know how to do some stuff with them. Like turn them on and open programs, play games and type, make drawings, and build Web pages—things like that. So I got up from my desk, pointed at the screen, and said, "Mrs. Snavin, if you double-click on that little thing right there, then the program will start running. And then you click on this, and that opens up the part about number lines."

So Mrs. Snavin did what I told her to and the program started running. Because that's the way it works and anybody knows that. Except Mrs. Snavin.

When the program started playing this stupid music, Mrs. Snavin smiled this huge smile at me and said, "Jake, you're *wonderful!*" And she said it too loud. *Way* too loud.

She said it so loud that every kid in the classroom

stopped and turned to look at us, just in time to see Mrs. Snavin pat me on the top of my head like I was a nice little poodle or something. An embarrassed poodle with a bright red face.

So I mumbled something like, "Oh, it was nothing." Which was a mistake.

Because right away she said, "But you're wrong, Jake. I get *so* mixed up when I work with these new computers. And to think that all along I've had such a *wonderful* expert right here in my classroom, and I didn't even know it! From now on you're going to be my *special* computer helper!"

I sat down fast before she could pat me on the head again. But the worst part hadn't happened yet. Because Mrs. Snavin walked to the front of the room and said, "Class, if any of you has trouble with the computers during math time this afternoon, just ask Jake what to do. He's my *special* computer helper!"

By this time, my face was so red that I felt my ears start to get hot. I kept my eyes on my desk but even so, I knew everyone in the room was looking at me. And I was just waiting for someone to start making fun of me, especially the kids who know tons more about computers than I do. Like Ben. Or

Shelley Orcut. She's the biggest computer brain in our whole school.

But just then the first period bell rang and it was time to go to art class. So I was saved by the bell.

Miss Cott's room was a big mess that morning. That's probably why I've always liked the art room so much. It's the one place at school where you don't have to worry about neatness. Or spilling stuff. Or getting everything done in a hurry.

The first thing we did in art class was put on our giant shirts. They're supposed to keep paint and glue and junk off our clothes. I put on an old blue shirt of my dad's. The other kids put on their giant shirts too, so we all looked like our legs had shrunk. Which is another fun thing about art class.

So on that Monday I went to work at an easel near the windows. We were supposed to be making pictures for Mother's Day.

I was about half done with my painting when I decided I needed a smaller brush. So I went to the big sink to get one. About fifteen or twenty brushes were sticking out of a bucket full of brownish greenish yellowish water. I grabbed a handful of brushes and looked for one that was the right size. Then I felt someone come up behind me. So I hurried up and rinsed off all the brushes under the faucet, took the one I wanted, and stuck the rest on the rack above the sink.

I looked behind me, and Miss Cott was standing there. She had this goofy look on her face, and her head was tilted to one side, and she was smiling. At me.

"Jake! That is the *sweetest* thing anybody has done in this room all week!" Which didn't make sense since it was only Monday morning and there hadn't been much of a week yet. But I guess that didn't matter to Miss Cott.

I gave this lame little smile and said, "I . . . I need a smaller brush so I can finish . . ."

Miss Cott said, "And instead of working to finish your picture, you've stopped to help clean up the brushes! That is so *sweet!*" By then, the whole class was watching us, and I was wishing that Miss Cott would stop saying *"sweet"* like that.

But Miss Cott wasn't done. She turned to all the kids in my class and said, "If all of you would be as *sweet* as Jake is and help clean up a little, then maybe this room wouldn't be such a mess all the time. Thank you *so much*, Jake!"

And as she said that, Miss Cott patted me on the head.

I took my small brush and hurried back to my easel. I started working on my picture again, trying not to feel so embarrassed.

Then I heard Ben whisper something to Mark. In addition to being great with computers, Ben Grumson was probably the meanest kid in my third-grade class. So he whispered extra loud so I'd be sure to hear him. "Hey Mark, don't you think Jake is just about perfect? He's so *sweet!*" I pretended not to hear, but I know my face turned redder and redder.

After art, we went back to our classroom for reading and social studies and nothing much happened.

Then right before lunch, we had gym class. Mr. Collins was having one of his tough-guy days. You can tell when Mr. Collins is having a tough-guy day because on tough-guy days, he calls all the boys and girls "troops."

After the bell rang, Mr. Collins blew his whistle and shouted, "Okay, troops, listen up. Get in a straight line here at the middle of the court. Come on, troops, look alive! Today we're going to play . . . dodgeball!"

Half the class groaned, and the other half cheered.

The kids who always get whomped by that fat, red ball groaned, and the kids who are great at throwing and catching cheered. I was one of the kids who groaned. For me, dodgeball means trying to stay alive.

Mr. Collins clapped his hands. "All right, troops! Everyone whose last name starts with A through L, over to the far side of the court. M through Z, over here behind me. Let's hustle! Go, go, go!"

Mr. Collins started the game by rolling the ball along the black line down the middle of the gym. Glen Purdy ran out and grabbed the ball for the other team.

There's something . . . weird about dodgeball. I don't know why it brings out the worst in some kids, but it does. Take Glen Purdy, for example. In real life, Glen is a pretty good kid. He's friendly, he's a good partner in math or reading, and he's good to have on your side in a basketball game because he's so tall.

But when a game of dodgeball starts up, all of a sudden this nice guy turns into a beast. And his arms are so long that when Glen throws that fat, red ball, it's like it was shot from a cannon.

So Glen had the ball, and right away, our whole team backed all the way against the wall. We knew that Glen was going to whomp someone. And he did.

Me. Right on the shoulder.

It took only about four minutes for the rest of my team to get knocked out, and then Mr. Collins clapped his hands and said, "Let's go, troops, another round, and this time it's a two-ball game."

And he rolled both balls along the black center line.

Which meant that now it was possible for some kid to get whomped with *two* fat, red balls at the same time. And that's what happened. To me. On the first throw. Again. I got one ball on the ankle and one ball in the stomach.

Here's what the next four games of dodgeball were like for me that day: *WHOMP! WHOMP! WHOMP! WHOMP!* Six games of dodgeball, and I was the first kid to get knocked out in every one of them.

But did I ask if I could go to the nurse when the third *WHOMP* knocked me down and I skinned my knee? No. And did I ask if I could lie down on the mats when the fifth *WHOMP* got me right on the head and made me see little rainbows all over the place? No. How come? Maybe because I was being stupid. But it's probably because I'm not that big so even if I get hurt sometimes, I don't want anybody to think I'm a quitter.

Anyway, I was so glad when that gym class was

finally over that I was the first in line at the door to be dismissed for lunch.

Mr. Collins came over to the doorway. He gave a blast on his whistle to quiet everyone down. Then he said, "Listen up, troops. You all played great today. Good job. But the Player of the Day, maybe the Player of the Month Award goes to a special guy. Did everyone see who took the first hit in every game today? Did that person complain? No. Did he whine and groan? No. Why? Because he's a real trooper, that's why. Jake Drake here deserves my Gym Class Medal of Honor, and you can all take some lessons from him on how to be a good sport. All right, troops—Dismissed!"

And of course, as Mr. Collins was talking about me, what was he doing? He was patting me on the head. And as he was talking, I was looking at the other kids, and I could tell they didn't think I should be getting all this attention just because I stink at dodgeball.

Standing there at the door of the gym with Mr. Collins patting me on the head, I got this sinking feeling in the pit of my stomach.

Because Monday was only half over, and I was already well on my way to becoming the most unpopular kid in the history of Despres Elementary School.

CHAPTER TWO

GARBAGE GUY

I went to my classroom after gym to grab my lunch bag, and then I hurried to the cafeteria. I wanted to sit with Willie. He's my best friend. His real name is Phil but his last name is Willis, so everyone calls him Willie. He was in Mrs. Frule's class when we were in third grade, so I only got to see him at lunch and at recess.

"Hi, Willie." I put my lunch on the table, and then went to get in the milk line.

Standing there, I looked over at a table and saw two girls from my class, Marsha and Jane. Marsha was looking at me and whispering something to Jane.

Then Jane looked at me, then they looked at each other, and then they both started laughing. I didn't like them laughing that way, but there was nothing I could do about it, so I got milk for Willie and me and went to sit down.

As I was walking back to my seat, I had to go past Ben Grumson. He was standing at the end of the lunch line with Karl Burton. And when I went past Ben, he grinned at Karl and said, "Hey look, it's Jake. He's a real *trooper*, y'know. And *sweet*, too." Karl laughed, even though he's one of my friends. I don't blame him. I guess it *was* pretty funny. Except not to me, not at that moment. I just gritted my teeth and walked back to Willie's table.

Willie nodded toward Ben and said, "What was that about?"

"That?" I said. "Nothing much. I got hit out first in dodgeball six times in a row in gym today. And then Mr. Collins made a big deal about it. So Ben was teasing me."

Willie made a face. "How can you stand being in Ben's class? He's such a jerk."

"Yeah," I agreed, "he is."

But then we started talking about this computer

game we wanted to get so we could link up our computers at home and play against each other. So lunch was great because Willie is always fun to talk to, and because I didn't have to worry about getting whomped on the side of the head by a fat, red ball.

When our cookies were gone, I said, "Let's go." With me and Willie, that meant it was time to play Rock, Paper, Scissors. Because every day after lunch we play three games of Rock, Paper, Scissors to see who has to carry our garbage to the trash barrel.

I won the first game, but Willie won the next two. He smiled and said, "I have to take a book back to the library, so maybe I'll see you after school."

I started to clean up. Willie is not what you would call a neat eater. His orange peels were all over the place, and he had flipped some potato chips around when he popped the bag open. Plus he had spilled some chocolate milk.

So I was standing up, leaning across the table, wiping up milk with some napkins, when all of a sudden, right behind me, I heard the sound that scares the daylights out of every kid at Despres Elementary School.

"YOU THERE!"

My heart just about jumped out of my mouth.

Because only one person at my school has a voice like that, and that's Mrs. Karp, the principal.

"Stop that, put that stuff down, and stand up straight!" Mrs. Karp was almost yelling, so the whole cafeteria got completely quiet. She has the kind of voice that makes kindergartners cry. It's so loud that I think she could break windows if she really shouted.

Mrs. Karp came over and stood right next to me. She looked around to make sure that everyone in the cafeteria was paying attention, and then with her huge voice said, "Every day, our cafeteria helpers have to spend extra time after lunch cleaning up in here. Take a good look at this table." She pointed at the mess in front of me—two ripped-up lunch bags, a squished chocolate-milk carton, three bent straws, a wad of soggy napkins, and a pile of orange peels and potato chips. It was not a pretty picture. I gulped, frozen with fear. Then Mrs. Karp said, "Jake Drake has not only started to clean up his own things, but he was also cleaning up the mess left behind by some *bad* citizen."

I looked up, and over by the door I saw Willie standing there—Willie the bad citizen. He made this scared face at me, like maybe he thought I was going to point at him and say, *There he is! He's the*

table trasher! But I would never do that.

Mrs. Karp had something in her hand. It was one of those patrol belts, the kind crossing guards wear. She leaned over toward me, and before I could do anything, she looped the strap over my head, pulled the belt around my waist, and hooked it together. It was way too big for me, so it sagged all over. Then she smiled and said, "See this patrol belt?" Which was a stupid question, because the thing is bright orange. It's impossible *not* to see it. "This week we're all going to make a special effort to keep our lunchroom clean. Jake Drake is going to wear this belt during lunch for the rest of the week. That will help to remind all of us not to leave *any* trash on our tables. And I want everyone to give Jake a nice round of applause for being such a fine lunchroom citizen. Jake, you've set a good example for everyone!"

And then Mrs. Karp started clapping and looking around the cafeteria, so everyone else had to clap too. And I saw Willie, over in the doorway, clapping like mad and grinning at me.

And once everyone was clapping, what did Mrs. Karp do? She stopped clapping, she reached over, and with all the kids in the third, fourth, and fifth grades watching, she patted me on the head.

The clapping ended, and after she smiled at me once more, Mrs. Karp walked away. I finished cleaning up the lunch table, and tried not to feel like everyone was looking at me. Which is not easy when you're wearing a big, floppy, orange patrol belt. I got out of the cafeteria fast.

Willie was waiting for me in the hallway. He pointed at the orange belt and pretended like it was something amazing. He opened his eyes up real wide and said, "Gee! Can I touch that?"

I didn't smile. I walked past him because I had to get back to Mrs. Snavin's room fast so I could take off the stupid thing and stick it inside my desk.

Willie caught up and said, "Don't get mad, Jake. I'm just kidding."

"Well, it's not funny," I said. I didn't like what was happening.

When lunch period was over, all the kids in my class went back to our room and we sat down and got out our math workbooks. Mrs. Snavin waited until all the kids got quiet and sat in their seats. Then she said, "Before we start on math, I need someone to take this note down to the office for me."

Right away, about six kids put up their hands, because some kids love to do that kind of stuff. Mrs. Snavin looked right past all those waving hands. She looked right at me and she smiled and said, "I think I'll have Jake take it." She held out the note toward me, so I had to get up from my seat, walk to the front of the room, and get it from her. Then Mrs. Snavin said, "But be sure to hurry right back, Jake, because we're going to work on our number-line project, and you have to be my *special* computer helper, okay?" And I could feel every kid in the class looking at me. They weren't saying anything. They weren't even whispering. But right then, I heard what they were thinking anyway. They were thinking, *teacher's pet.*

And Mrs. Snavin didn't help. All during the last two hours of the day, she kept asking me to remind her how to do different things on the computer or to go over and help this kid and then help that kid. And the worst part was that nobody really needed help and they didn't want help, especially from the *teacher's pet.* And Mrs. Snavin came and watched me when it was my turn to use the computer, and she said, "It's so wonderful to see a real *expert* use this math program!" I thought the day would never end.

But it did. When I finally ran outside to wait for my bus, I was in a pretty bad mood. And when I was standing in line, a fifth-grade boy went by and said, "Hey, Garbage Guy! I think Mrs. Karp is in love with you!"

And then all his friends laughed and another kid said, "Yeah—Garbage Guy! Maybe you can clean up *my* lunch table tomorrow. And do a good job, because you don't want to make the principal unhappy!"

Bus number three came and I got on. I sat on the outside edge of a seat so no one could sit with me. I didn't want to talk to anyone. I just sat there, staring at the dirty black floor. All around me kids were talking and joking, yelling and laughing. Not me.

I felt terrible. It wasn't fair. I didn't want to be a teacher's pet. I didn't try to get anybody's attention. It wasn't my fault. I felt like I was trapped.

I looked up and my stop was next. When the bus stopped, I jumped up and got to the front of the bus. I wanted to be the first one off. I was ready for this day to be over.

It was real noisy, and the lady driving the bus turned around in her seat and shouted, "Quiet!"

When everybody stopped yelling and talking, the driver looked around and said, "You kids have got to settle down! It's not safe to drive when it gets so loud and crazy. You should all be sitting still in your seats, and if you talk at all, you talk quietly, understand? On this whole bus, only one kid has been a good bus rider today—and that's this kid right here."

And with all the kids on the bus watching her, the bus driver reached over and patted me on the head.

CHAPTER THREE

SPECIAL TREATMENT

When I got home that afternoon, I walked right up to my room. I didn't even get a snack.

That's how come my mom followed me. She came into my room and said, "Jake, is everything all right?"

I didn't know how to explain. Because if I said to her, "All of my teachers, and even the principal, all think I'm wonderful," then my mom would say something like, "Well, you *are* wonderful, Jake!" Because that's what moms do.

So I said, "I'm okay, Mom. I just got kind of tired at school today." Which was true. Having every kid in the school think you're trying to be the teacher's pet makes you tired. And being whomped six or seven times by a dodgeball doesn't help either.

But after dinner we got to watch this really good TV show about the Coast Guard, and so I stopped thinking about school and I felt better.

After Dad read a chapter of our book at bedtime, and after he tucked me in and kissed me good night and turned out my light, I couldn't help thinking about school again. The way I finally got to sleep was by telling myself it was probably just a bad Monday. I told myself that tomorrow, everything would go back to normal. Tomorrow, I would just be a regular kid again. That's what I told myself, and I hoped it would be true. I wanted it to be true. I needed it to be true. And I went to sleep believing it.

Tuesday's bus ride to school was great. I was just a kid. Not too loud, not too quiet. The bus driver didn't even notice I was there, and no one said a word about anything that had happened on Monday. And I said to myself, *See? Nothing to worry about.*

But I spoke too soon. The second I walked into her room, Mrs. Snavin said, "Oh, good! You're here,

Jake. I don't know how I'll ever survive another day without my *special* computer helper!" Then she pointed at her computer screen and said, "I've got that math program open, and I'm afraid it's all muddled again. Would you come over here and see if I've done this right?" She hadn't done it right, so I had to fix it for her. And when I was done, Mrs. Snavin said, "Jake, you've saved my life again!"

By that time, almost all the other kids were in the classroom. I could feel them looking at me, and I could tell they were thinking, *There's the teacher's pet, already hard at work.*

And it really looked that way. Because who did Mrs. Snavin pick to take the attendance sheet down to the office? Me. And during reading period, who did Mrs. Snavin call on first to read out loud? Me. And who did Mrs. Snavin choose to be first in line to go to an assembly in the auditorium? Me.

Everyone had been looking forward to that assembly for a while. It was this lady who called herself Miss Thumbelina the Storyteller. She had performed at our school before, and she was great. She told stories, but she didn't just read them. She acted out all the parts all by herself. She had a bunch of different costumes and hats and beards and wigs, and huge baskets full of things like swords and ropes and lanterns. If there was a castle in a story, then she'd pull a chunk of a castle wall out of a basket and make you believe the whole castle was right there.

I was glad Miss Thumbelina was performing that Tuesday. It was only ten-thirty, but already I needed a break. I wanted to sit in a huge room in the middle of all the kids from grades three, four, and five. Then the auditorium would get dark, and I could disappear into the crowd and enjoy the show.

Miss Thumbelina came onto the stage and we all started clapping. She had on this wig with long red hair. She made a low bow, and then she said, "Good morning! I'm going to start our program today with an old, old story. To help me tell this story, I need a helper, someone who's loyal and true and honest and good, a real knight in shining armor." And then she held one hand up to her forehead to shade her eyes from the bright lights, and with her other hand she pointed out into the audience.

And she pointed at a fourth grader sitting right in front of me. "You there!" she said. "You look like a prince to me! Come on up onstage and help me tell

this tale!" The kid started to shake his head no, and I felt sorry for him.

Suddenly Mrs. Snavin was there next to me. She said, "Jake! You're the *perfect* one to help her!" And she said it way too loud. She grabbed me by the arm and pulled me up out of my seat. When Miss Thumbelina saw me standing up, she clapped her hands and said, "Great! Here comes our prince!"

Fifteen seconds later I was walking across the stage, blinking like crazy and trying not to trip on the stuff that was everywhere.

There's no way to get ready for the worst ten minutes of your life. One minute I was sitting in the dark enjoying the show, and the next minute, I *was* the show, and this lady in a big wig was sticking a knight's helmet on my head and strapping plastic armor around my chest. Then she handed me a long sword, which would have been fun to mess with if four hundred kids hadn't been laughing at me.

Then Miss Thumbelina put this thing around me that was supposed to be a horse. There was a horse's head in front and a horse's rump and tail in back, and there was a place for me in the middle. The whole thing hung from my shoulders by two straps. To make the horse go, I had to run like this: *ba-da bum, ba-da bum, ba-da bum.*

As she hooked me into the horse she said, "Now, here's all you have to do: Wait behind the curtains, and whenever I say, 'Someone will save me!', you come galloping all the way across the stage, right past me. And you wave your sword and yell, 'I'll save you, Princess!' Then you go behind the curtains on the far side and wait there. And when I say that line again, you run out and do the same thing, okay?"

I nodded and said, "Okay," because I was already strapped into the costume, and the lady was ready to start. What else could I do?

I hid behind the curtain and Miss Thumbelina started telling her story. The way the story went, she said, "Someone will save me!" about twenty times. Then this dopey knight would gallop across the stage yelling, "I'll save you, Princess!"—that was the big joke. That was me. I was the big dopey joke.

Finally, the story was over. Miss Thumbelina made me and my horse come to the center of the stage. I had to hold her hand and take a bow. Then I galloped over behind the curtain and I got out of that costume in about three seconds.

I think I set a new record for blushing that day. Even though there was a show up on the stage, every time I looked around, it felt like half the kids in the auditorium were looking at me. So I tried not to notice. And it worked, because after a while I forgot about my terrible time on the stage, and I just watched the rest of the stories like everyone else.

At the end of the last story, everybody clapped like crazy. It really was a great assembly. All the teachers stood up, and Mrs. Karp walked onto the stage. She held up her hands and the clapping stopped.

Mrs. Karp said, "I know I speak for everyone when I tell Miss Thumbelina how much we all enjoyed her performance today. Let's all give her one last round of applause."

So we all started clapping and cheering again. Then Mrs. Karp held up her hands again, and the noise stopped, just like turning off a TV.

Mrs. Karp said, "And before I forget, Jake, would you come back up onstage?"

The whole auditorium got quiet except for some scattered giggling. I turned bright red and walked up onto the stage. Mrs. Karp motioned for me to come and stand beside her. Then she said, "I think we should also give a nice round of applause to our young man of many talents, our own Jake Drake!" And as she said my name, she reached down and patted me on the head.

I'm not sure who started it, but I think it was Ben Grumson. Because when the kids started clapping, someone began saying, "Jake Drake, Jake Drake, Jake Drake," and every kid in the room picked up on it. Four hundred kids started chanting my name.

Then the strangest thing I've ever seen happened. Instead of frowning and stopping the chanting like she could have, Mrs. Karp smiled, and started clapping her hands, and she chanted along with the kids: "Jake Drake, Jake Drake, Jake Drake!"

I couldn't believe it. I felt like I was in a movie where aliens had taken over a school and made everyone act completely nuts.

After all the kids and teachers and Mrs. Karp had chanted my name about fifteen times, it was starting to feel like the roof might blow off the auditorium. Finally, Mrs. Karp held up her hands and right away the noise stopped. Because even in the middle of a riot, no one would ever mess around with Mrs. Karp.

And then the principal dismissed us to go back to

our classrooms and get ready for lunch, like nothing strange had happened at all.

So I tried to act that way too. I kept my eyes on the floor and went back toward our classroom. And when some kid in the hallway started chanting, "Jake Drake, Jake Drake, Jake Drake," I didn't look up. I just kept walking.

I was so glad to be back in my own classroom. It was going to be so good to go to lunch and sit down in a quiet corner with Willie.

I opened my desk to get my lunch, and I gasped. A bunch of kids turned to look at me. I must have sounded like I had seen a ghost. Except it was scarier than that for me. Because I had forgotten. There, under my lunch bag was the most horrible thing I'd ever seen—that bright orange patrol belt!

I was not going to go have a quiet lunch with my best friend. For the second time in one hour, I was going to put on a costume and get on a stage. This time, I wasn't going to be a knight in shining armor. This time I had to put on a floppy, orange belt and walk into the cafeteria. Because every kid in grades three, four, and five was waiting for me. Everyone was waiting for Garbage Guy.

CHAPTER FOUR

DANGEROUS

I thought about just not wearing the orange patrol belt to lunch. I thought about it for three seconds or so. Then I remembered Mrs. Karp. She would be in the cafeteria too. And she had said I would wear the thing for the rest of the week. I guess she thought wearing the belt was supposed to be an honor. Maybe like having a black belt in karate. Except it wasn't.

So I pulled the thing out of my desk. I looped it over one shoulder, hooked it around my waist, grabbed my lunch, and went out into the hall. Right away a group of fourth-grade girls started to point at me and giggle. But I just held my head up high and walked toward the cafeteria. I kept walking, and I said to myself, *I can live through this. I know I can. I can do this.* And I just pretended that nothing was the matter.

When I got to the cafeteria, I looked for Willie, but he wasn't at our regular table. Then I saw him in the milk line. When I went over to say hi, Willie started talking to me like a spy. He kept looking straight ahead and he tried not to move his lips.

He whispered, "I can't eat with you today."

I whispered back, "How come?"

He said, "Mrs. Karp. She'll know it was me."

"What do you mean?" I asked.

Willie said, "Me. I left that big mess yesterday."

I said, "But I'll tell her we played Rock, Paper, Scissors, and I lost."

Willie shook his head. "Uh-uh. Better not. See you at recess."

And maybe Willie was right, because Mrs. Karp was already prowling around the lunchroom. She was on the lookout for trashers.

So I got some milk and went to find a place to sit. And as I looked around the cafeteria, it felt like there was a big sign at every table, and the sign said, "No Teacher's Pets Allowed."

Even the table where I usually sat with Willie was filled up. There was only one empty table. And there was a reason it was empty: It was the one next to the teachers' table. Because at our school the teachers get lunch for free. Except it's not really free. To get a free lunch they have to eat in the cafeteria when their class eats. That was Mrs. Karp's idea to help keep the lunchroom quieter.

So I went to the empty table and sat down. Alone. Just me and my orange patrol belt. And I said to myself, *I can live through this. I know I can. I can do this.*

I opened up my lunch bag, and that made me feel better right away. My mom had packed chocolate pudding *plus* Fig Newtons—two desserts! So I wanted to get the rest of my food out of the way fast. I had just taken a huge bite out of a bologna sandwich, when a voice behind me said, "Is this seat taken? The teachers' table is too crowded today."

It was Miss Cott, my art teacher. And before I could chew or swallow or say a word, she sat down right next to me, ripped the lid off a Tupperware tub, and started eating a salad that smelled like rotten eggs and onions. And she sat there. Next to me. When she wasn't jamming salad into her mouth, she was smiling at me and chatting away—like she was my best friend or something.

I stopped chewing and looked around the room. About half the kids in the cafeteria were staring at me. Staring at us. At me and Miss Cott. And I could see what they were thinking. It was all over their faces, as plain as grape jelly: *Jake Drake is such a teacher's pet that he even eats lunch with one!*

I finished my sandwich and then ate my two desserts so fast I didn't even taste them. Then I looked sideways at Miss Cott and said, "Gotta go," and before she could say anything, I grabbed my garbage and left. I went straight across the room, dumped my trash, and went out the side door to the playground.

The first thing I did outside was take off the orange belt and stuff it into my pocket. Because Mrs. Karp never said I had to wear it during recess.

Willie waved at me from the other side of the playground, and I ran over to meet him. The sun was shining, the sky was blue, and birds were singing. It was a beautiful May afternoon, it was recess, and I had survived lunch. I started to feel okay again.

Just before I got to Willie, three fifth graders jumped off the jungle gym and caught up to me.

I stopped and said, "Hi."

The biggest kid looked familiar, but I didn't know his name. He gave me this mean smile and said, "Hey, Garbage Guy—better put your little belt back on. I think I see some trash over there by the fence."

Then the one who was wearing a baseball hat said, "Yeah, and maybe you should get your fake horsie and ride it around the playground for us."

They laughed and high-fived each other, and all three of them got closer and started chanting: "Jake Drake! Jake Drake! Jake Drake! Jake Drake!" Then they got right up into my face. "Jake Drake! Jake Drake! Jake Drake! Jake Drake!" And I just couldn't take it. So I grabbed the guy with the baseball hat and pushed him as hard as I could right into the other two kids. They weren't ready for that, and all three of them lost their balance and fell down in a heap on the grass. And they stopped chanting my name.

They began to scramble around, trying to get up,

and I could see it was time to get out of there. I turned to run, but I bumped into someone. It was Mrs. Karp, standing right there, looking very tall and very angry.

"What's going on here? You boys, get up off the ground this instant!"

Those kids *had* been mean to me, but still, *I* was the one who pushed first. I was the one who had started fighting. So I said, "Mrs. Karp, I . . ."

And she said, "I know, Jake. You didn't have anything to do with this. Of course not." Then she frowned at the other kids. "You boys, follow me to the office. Now."

And as the fifth graders walked away behind Mrs. Karp, the one at the end of the line, the biggest one, turned to look at me. He narrowed his eyes and pointed at me, and I could see his mouth move. He didn't make a sound, but I saw what he said. He said, "I'm gonna get you!" And I didn't blame him. It wasn't fair. I was the one who started fighting, but Mrs. Karp didn't see it.

Willie came over and said, "That was awesome! I thought we were going to have to fight all three of them at once!"

I just nodded. Everything had happened so fast.

Willie said, "But I don't think I'd want to be you right now. That big kid? You know who he is, right?"

I shook my head, and Willie said, "No? You don't *know* who *that* is? That's Danny Grumson, Ben's big brother. He's only the toughest kid in the whole school, that's all!"

And standing there on the playground with Willie going on and on about Danny Grumson, something suddenly became very clear to me: Being a teacher's pet can be dangerous. Very dangerous.

CHAPTER FIVE

NO MORE MR. NICE GUY

The second I got on my bus that afternoon, three or four kids in the back started chanting, "Jake Drake! Jake Drake! Jake Drake!" They probably would have done it forever, but the bus driver turned around and made them stop.

I sat on a seat by myself. Alone. Just like at lunch, but without Miss Cott.

When I got off the bus, I walked the rest of the way to my house. Alone.

And I didn't feel like a snack, so I went up to my room and I shut the door and flopped flat on my back onto my bed. Alone.

I was feeling pretty sorry for myself. And lying there on my bed, I said what I always say when I feel sorry for myself. I said, "It's not fair!"

And it wasn't. I didn't want to be a teacher's pet. It just happened. I helped Mrs. Snavin with the computer—*Bam!*—teacher's pet. I washed out a couple of paintbrushes—*Bam!*—teacher's pet. I got whomped in gym—*Bam!*—teacher's pet. Cleaned up trash, didn't yell on the bus, helped that storyteller—*Bam! Bam! Bam!*—teacher's pet.

The teachers and even the principal—all of them thought I was so special, so wonderful.

I sat up on my bed. Was I so special and wonderful? Of course not! No Way. *But*, if that's what all my teachers *thought*, then that's how they were going to treat me. I'd be *special*, and *sweet*, a real *trooper.*

It was so simple. If my teachers thought I was always so wonderful and so nicey-nice, I'd just have to prove they were making a mistake.

Suddenly I felt great. I jumped off my bed and ran downstairs to get a snack. In the pantry I found a bag of chocolate-chip cookies and I piled about ten of them onto a plate. Then I poured myself a big glass

of milk but the carton was really full and I spilled milk all over the counter. I started to grab a paper towel to wipe it up—but then I stopped myself.

I smiled and I dunked a cookie into my glass and I crunched it, and I let the crumbs fall all over the place. And when I was done eating cookies and spraying crumbs around, I just left everything a mess. I didn't even put the milk back into the refrigerator. And I said to myself, *Now, if this was tomorrow and I was at school, I'd just walk away and leave all this!*

I grinned as I cleaned up the counter and put the milk away. Thinking like that was good practice.

Because tomorrow I wasn't going to be good and clean up after myself. I was going to be bad and rude and unpleasant and messy.

Because on Wednesday, everybody at school was going to see a different Jake Drake.

CHAPTER SIX

BAD JAKE

On Wednesday morning as I got on the bus, the driver watched me climb up the steps.

When I was right next to her, she gave me a big smile and said, "How's my favorite little bus rider today?"

I frowned at her and I said, "Terrible. And this bus smells bad!"

The lady got this shocked look on her face. Then she pushed her lips together, turned her face away, and looked up into her big mirror. She shouted, "Hurry up and sit down back there!" Then she slammed the doors shut and grabbed the steering wheel.

As I sat down, I didn't know if I should feel bad or smile. But the important thing was this: That was one bus driver who wasn't going to think Jake Drake was so nicey-nice anymore. And I thought, *Maybe she'll even send me to the principal's office for being rude!* And I was happy about that.

Because that Wednesday, I had to be someone else, someone different. I was going to make some trouble.

When I got off the bus, Willie was waiting for me. We started walking toward the playground because it wasn't time to go inside yet.

This first-grade boy ran right in front of us, and I stuck out my foot. The kid stumbled and rolled onto the grass.

"Hey!" he yelled. And he got up and said, "That wasn't nice!"

I made this mean face at him, and I said, "Yeah? So what?"

The kid was pretty little, so he just frowned and started running again.

Willie looked at me funny. "You okay?"

I said, "No, I'm not okay. All the teachers think I'm so nice, and all the kids think I'm a big teacher's pet." Then I stopped walking and I looked at Willie.

I said, "That's what they think, don't they?"

Willie scrunched up his face. "Well . . . I didn't want to say anything, but, yeah. I heard some kids in my class talking about you yesterday. They said you want all the teachers to think you're perfect. They said . . . they said you make them sick. I . . . I was going to tell them it wasn't true, but then Mrs. Frule looked at us so we had to shut up."

I said, "Well, don't worry about it. Because I'm going to do something about all that. Today."

Willie looked puzzled. "What do you mean?"

"I mean, I'm going to show everybody that I'm not a teacher's pet, that's what."

"But how?" asked Willie.

"I'm just not going to be so nice."

"You mean, like . . . like tripping that kid?" asked Willie. And when I nodded, he said, "But . . . if you do stuff like that, you're gonna get in trouble."

I looked at Willie. And I smiled and nodded my head again.

And Willie smiled too. "Ohhh . . . I get it."

Then the bell rang and kids started for the doors.

Willie said, "Well, have a good day. I mean, have a *bad* day!"

And I grinned and said, "*Real* bad!"

When I got to Mrs. Snavin's room, I threw my jacket into the bottom of my cubby, and then tossed my backpack onto the floor by my desk.

I sat down in my chair and pulled a comic book out of my backpack. I had never read a comic book at school before. It was kind of fun.

When she saw me, Mrs. Snavin came to the back of the room and sat down at the computer closest to my desk. She turned it on and fiddled with it for a minute or two. Then she said, "Jake, this math program is acting up again."

I kept reading my comic book. I pretended not to hear her.

She kept tapping on keys, and then she put her hands in her lap and let out a big sigh. "Jake?" I could tell Mrs. Snavin was looking right at me. "Jake, what should I do?"

Without looking away from my comic book I said, "Take a computer class." That's what I said. Rude. Unhelpful. And I said it loud enough so every kid in the class could hear me.

The room got very quiet. My hands were sweating, and my fingers made spots on the paper of the comic book. Mrs. Snavin was getting furious, I was sure of it. She was getting ready to yell at me, tell me to put away the junk I was reading.

Five seconds passed.

Then Mrs. Snavin stood up slowly and walked over to my desk. I felt her standing there, a little too close. I gulped, ready for the worst. She reached out her hand to grab my comic book.

Except she didn't.

Instead, she patted me on the head. "Jake, you are *absolutely* right! I've just been putting it off and putting it off, and now, thanks to you, that's *just* what I'm going to do. I'm going to sign up for a computer class today this *very* afternoon! Because if I can't run the computers in my own classroom, then I guess I have no business using them. So we'll just forget about the computers for a while. After all, who says we need computers to learn about number lines anyway? I have stacks and stacks of perfectly good worksheets. Jake, you're *wonderful!* I don't know what I'd do without you!"

Ben Grumson gave me this dirty look. And so did about twenty other kids. Because now instead of using the computers for math, we were going to have to do worksheets. I mean, the math game was pretty stupid, but we still got to use a computer. Which is a lot better than worksheets.

Then Mrs. Snavin said, "Jake, could you to go to the office for me and ask Mrs. Drinkwater for the community college catalog?"

I just kept reading my comic book, and I said, "I'm reading." Not nice at all. My hands were still sweating.

And what does Mrs. Snavin say? Does she say, "Listen here, young man! You put down that trash and do what I tell you to!"? Does she grab me by the arm and say, "I don't like the tone of your voice, Mr. Drake! We better talk to the principal about this!"?

No. Right away Mrs. Snavin says, "Why of course. How *rude* of me. Here you are doing some extra reading before class even starts, and I'm interrupting you. You've always been such a *good* reader! I'll send someone else." And she did.

That's when I decided I would have to try harder. I wasn't being bad enough.

After attendance and the Pledge of Allegiance, Mrs. Snavin said, "All right, class. For reading today, let's begin by talking about the story we finished yesterday. Let's see . . . Karl, what's one thing you liked about 'Tom's Pet Crow'?"

Karl sat up straighter in his chair and said, "Well, I kind of liked the way Tom taught the crow how to . . ."

Right while Karl was talking, I just butted in, and I said, "I didn't like anything about that story."

Mrs. Snavin's eyebrows went up. "Nothing? My goodness, Jake. You shouldn't have interrupted Karl . . . but maybe you should tell us one thing you *didn't* like."

I said, "The whole story was stupid. And boring. And I didn't like it. At all."

"Well!" said Mrs. Snavin. "How about the rest of you? Is there anyone else who didn't like the story?"

I looked around, and almost every kid's hand went up in the air. And I thought, *Hey! Look! I'm a leader! They agree with me. And they can see that I'm not the teacher's pet! Hurrah!*

Mrs. Snavin looked around, and then she looked at me, and she took a deep breath and let it out slowly. And I thought, *Uh-oh. Now I'm going to get it!*

Then she smiled. At me. And she said, "Jake, you are *so* right! I didn't like this story very much, either. That'll teach me to pay more attention to what's good and what's not! So let's skip ahead in

51

our reading books . . . all the way to page 287."

While we were flipping pages, Mrs. Snavin said, "Now, this is a longer story, so you won't have time to finish it during reading time. But you can take it home and finish it tonight. And I hope you'll like this story better, because, like Jake says, a story should never be boring or stupid. Right now, I want everyone to take out a piece of paper and write down three ways you think 'Tom's Pet Crow' could be better."

All around the class, kids were groaning and giving me dirty looks. Because now we had to do some writing. *And* we had homework, *and* it was all my fault. Plus, Mrs. Snavin was still smiling at me and saying how smart I was.

And I was starting to wonder, *How bad do I have to be to make her stop treating me like her little sweetie pie?* Because being bad isn't as easy as some kids make it look.

A little later during art class, Miss Cott came over and looked at the painting I was making for Mother's Day. She stood there a minute, and then she said, "Jake, that is so *sweet*! I think that's just about the *sweetest* Mother's Day painting I've ever seen!"

Before art, I didn't know how I was going to be

bad in Miss Cott's class. But when she said that, I knew just what to do. I grabbed the bottom of my painting and I pulled the paper out of the clips on the easel. I ripped it up and I said, "Well, I think it's a rotten painting!" Real loud. And then I grabbed the little brush I had been using and I snapped it right in half.

Miss Cott stood there with her mouth open. Every kid in the class was looking at her, waiting for an explosion. Then she took a deep breath and sat down in a chair. She started nodding her head. Then in a soft voice she said, "Class, I want you all to pay attention." Which is something she didn't need to say. She was still nodding her head. I thought she was going to start screaming any second. She looked around at the class and said, "Jake has just been *very* brave. You see, I said I liked his painting, and what did Jake do? He tore it up! He *knows* he can do better work than that, and he's not afraid to tear up his work and start over! Jake, I think you might be the *best* art student in this whole school!" And then Miss Cott smiled at me like I had just painted the Mona Lisa or something. So art class was a bust. I was still the teacher's pet.

One of Mr. Collins's big rules is "Never Swing on the Ropes." So what did I do at the beginning of gym

class? I swung on the ropes, and I yelled, "Yahoooo!" while I was doing it. And when Mr. Collins came through the doorway and saw me, what did he do? Did he come and grab me? Did he shake his fist at me? No. He grinned. Then he said, "I was wondering who'd be the first kid to break that rule this year. I love a kid who's got some *spirit,* some *backbone!* The rest of you kids could take a lesson from Drake here. Okay, trooper, off that rope, and give me five push-ups. And the next kid who swings will do thirty push-ups *and* thirty sit-ups, so the rest of you, don't get any ideas."

Then at lunch when I handed the orange belt to Mrs. Karp and said, "I don't want to wear this anymore," did I get in trouble? No. Mrs. Karp patted me on the head and announced something to everyone in the cafeteria. She smiled at me and said Jake Drake was being very unselfish. She said Jake Drake wanted to share the *fun* of wearing the lunch patrol belt with someone else. And then she gave the belt to Ben Grumson. Who did not smile at me.

And no one was happy with me during afternoon math time, either, because we all had to do three worksheets. Instead of using the computers. Because of me.

So by the end of school on Wednesday afternoon, I was ready to give up. All day I had been about as bad and rude as I knew how to be. And it hadn't done any good. I was still the teacher's pet. *Every* teacher's pet.

After school as I got on the bus, this wave of lemon smell rolled down the stairs at me. Then I saw three yellow air fresheners hanging from the back of the driver's seat. Before I could get past her, the bus driver grabbed me and gave me a big hug.

She said, "After what you said this morning, well, I went right out and bought these things for the bus. And when I went to take care of my little grandson today, he climbed up on my lap and he said, 'Gamma mells good!' Isn't that the cutest thing you ever heard?!" Then the lady hugged me again. With everyone watching. And she said, "You're still my favorite little passenger!"

No doubt about it: I had a one-way ticket to Petsville.

CHAPTER SEVEN

BAD DREAM, GOOD IDEA

Wednesday night I had a dream.

I was in a cage, a little wire cage in a room. I was on my hands and knees. There were two bowls inside my cage. One of them was filled with Cheerios and the other one had root beer. Every once in awhile I would bend down and eat a mouthful of cereal, and then lick up some root beer. All around me there were little cages with other kids in them. Mark was in one, and Ben Grumson, and there was Marsha, and Karl—even Willie. All of us were munching cereal and lapping up soda.

Then this tall lady came into the room. She bent

down and looked in every cage. She looked in Marsha's cage, and when she did, she frowned and said, "No!" Then she looked in at Ben, and she frowned and said, "No!" She looked into every cage and she kept saying, "No! No! No!"

Then she bent down and looked into my cage, and she smiled and said, "Yes!" And she opened my cage and put an orange dog collar around my neck. And she held out a Fig Newton and said, "Good boy!" And when I sat up, she put the Fig Newton in my mouth. I started to chew the Fig Newton. Then the tall lady bent down and patted me on the head. And she said, "Now you're my little pet!" And when I looked into the lady's face, it was Mrs. Karp!

I sat up in my bed and I grabbed at my neck and I started yelling, "No! No! Take this collar off me! I'm not your pet! No! Nooo!"

And that's when my dad came into my room and turned on the light.

"Easy, Jake, it's all right." Dad sat on my bed, and he held on to my arm. "It's all right, Jake. You were just having a dream, that's all. You're Jake, and I'm your dad, and we're right here in our own house, and you're awake now, and everything's all right." I

was shaking and I was all sweaty. And Dad kept holding on to my arm. I was so glad he was there.

When I was totally awake, Dad said, "Bad dream, huh?"

I nodded. "Yeah. A nightmare." And I shivered. Then I said, "Dad, were you ever a teacher's pet?"

He said, "Hmm. Let me think . . . yes, I think I was, once. Back when I was in sixth grade."

My eyes opened wide. "Really? Did you *want* to be?"

Dad smiled. "Did I want to be? Yes, I suppose I did. My English teacher was a lady named Mrs. Palmer, and she was very smart. And I guess I thought she was pretty, too. My friend Tim and I stayed after class sometimes to help erase the chalkboards and straighten up her room, little things like that. So, I guess we were *both* teacher's pets."

I frowned. "And did she treat you and your friend special? Or let you get away with stuff?"

Dad thought a second, and then nodded. "Yes, I think she did, at least a little bit. I remember one time when I didn't do my homework and Mrs. Palmer caught me. She frowned at me and scolded me in class and said I had to come in after school. But when I went after school, she just smiled and said,

'Now, you won't do that again, will you, Jimmy?' And I said, 'No,' and then she let me leave. And I always did my homework after that too."

"But what about the other kids?" I asked. "Didn't they hate you for being the teacher's pet?"

Dad scratched his head, which made his hair look even more messed up. He said, "I don't really remember. All I remember is how Mrs. Palmer used to smile at me sometimes."

I said, "But what if you had a lot of teachers, and they were all being super nice to you, and you didn't even like the way they smiled, and then all the kids thought you were trying to be all goody-goody. What about that?"

"Well . . ." And then Dad gave this really big yawn. "If I was *trying* to get the teachers to treat me special, then I guess the kids would be right. Because that would be like I was trying to get away with something. But if a teacher decides to be nicer to you than she is to some other kid, then that's not your fault. That's the teacher's fault. Because a teacher's not supposed to be nicer to one kid than she is to another, right?"

I nodded and Dad said, "Now listen. You lean back on your pillow, and shut your eyes and go back to sleep, all right?" And he pulled my covers up under my chin, and kissed me on the cheek, and then got up and shut off the light. "Good night, Jake."

"G'night, Dad."

"Sleep tight."

Then I was alone again. And I kept thinking. Because Dad was right. A teacher's not supposed to be nicer to one kid than she is to another. Or a principal, either. And I wasn't trying to be a teacher's pet. I was just being myself. So it wasn't my fault. And even when I had tried to be bad, that hadn't worked, either, because—because I'm *not* bad, and everyone knows it.

And then I got a big idea. It was big, and it was simple. But would it work? Maybe it was too simple.

There was only one way to find out. And only one place, too, and that was school. On Thursday. So first I had to go back to sleep. And that's what I did.

And I didn't have any more dreams about orange dog collars.

CHAPTER EIGHT

NOT SO SPECIAL

Trying out a new plan can be scary. But if you don't try it out, you can't find out if it's going to work.

So Thursday morning right after attendance and the Pledge of Allegiance and the announcements, I put my hand up and waited for Mrs. Snavin to call on me.

She said, "Yes, Jake?"

And I took a deep breath and I said, "Mrs. Snavin? You know how you were having trouble with the computers? Well, I think that if we wanted to use them for math today, then you should really ask Shelley. She knows a lot more about computers than I do. And Ben, too. He's good with programs. They could really help. Then maybe we could use the computers for math, even before you finish your computer class. Because they're a lot more fun to use than worksheets."

Mrs. Snavin said, "Maybe after reading there'll be some time to work on them. Does that sound good to everyone?"

And a lot of the kids in the class nodded and said, "Yes."

Then Mrs. Snavin said, "That was a good idea, Jake. Thank you." And she smiled at me.

And I didn't care if she smiled at me, because it *was* a good idea. And I didn't care if the whole class saw her smile at me, because there's nothing wrong with being glad about a good idea, right? And sharing a good idea didn't make me a teacher's pet, right? It just made me myself.

And that was my big idea. From the night before. To just be myself and not think about being a teacher's pet. Because if I know I'm *not* a teacher's pet, then I'm not. Right?

But it's tricky, because if you get treated special, everyone will still think you're a teacher's pet. That's what kids hate, when a kid gets treated special. Because it's not fair. And it's really not. Because a teacher is supposed to treat all the kids the same.

After reading, Mrs. Snavin had to send some lunch money to the office, and I asked her if I could take it. Not because I was a teacher's pet. I wanted to go to the office for another reason.

When I got to the office, I gave the money to the school secretary, and then I said, "Is Mrs. Karp busy?"

Mrs. Drinkwater looked at me from behind the counter and said, "Yes, Jake. Just sit down over there for a minute."

So I sat down and gulped, because even when you're not in trouble, waiting to see the principal is no fun.

A couple of minutes later, Mrs. Karp came out, and when she saw me, she got this big smile on her face. She said, "Come into my office, Jake." And when I did, she sat down. And I was glad she did. Mrs. Karp is so tall that she's extra scary until she sits down. Then she asked, "Now, what can I do for you?"

I gulped again, and I said, "I'm having a problem. Ever since Monday, things have been happening to

me. Things that make all the other kids think I'm a big teacher's pet."

Then I stopped to look at her face. I wanted to make sure she didn't look mad or anything. And she didn't, so I kept talking. "Because, I'm *not* a teacher's pet. I'm just a regular kid. But if everyone thinks I am, then that's bad, right?"

Mrs. Karp nodded her head slowly, and said, "Yes . . . I can see how that would be a problem. And teachers should not be giving special privileges to children. Are some teachers treating you special?"

And I said, "Well, kind of. Sometimes. I think."

And Mrs. Karp leaned forward in her chair and said, "Really? When? And who?"

And I gulped extra hard and I said, "Like on Tuesday. With . . . with you."

"What? What are you talking about?" Mrs. Karp looked kind of angry, but I couldn't stop in the middle.

So I told her. About me starting that fight on the playground, about pushing that fifth grader. And about how the other kids got in trouble and I didn't. Because she said she knew that it wasn't my fault. When it really was.

Mrs. Karp leaned back again and put her fingertips

together. "Ah. Yes. I can see how that would be a problem—even though I didn't see you push anyone. And before that, the assembly . . . and then the lunchroom business. My goodness! This has been quite a week for you, hasn't it, Jake?"

And I nodded and said, "Yeah. Really."

Mrs. Karp stood up and walked around her desk. "Well, you'd better get back to class, Jake. I'll do some thinking about this. Maybe we can talk some more at lunchtime."

"At lunchtime?" I asked. "Should I come to the office then?"

Mrs. Karp was quiet a moment, and then she said, "No. I'll come and find you, all right? And I'm glad you were brave enough to come and talk to me."

And I could tell Mrs. Karp kind of wanted to pat me on the head. But she didn't. And I was glad.

When I got back to the classroom, it was free period. Some kids were reading, some were drawing or building with LEGO blocks, and Shelley and Ben were working on the computers.

I went back and stood next to Ben, looking over his shoulder at the screen. When he saw me I asked, "Fixed it yet?"

He didn't take his eyes off the screen. "Yeah. It was simple. But I'm pretending it's real hard. That way, I might get to come in over lunchtime. Then I can play a game." Ben took his hand off the keys and reached into his pocket. Looking around to be sure Mrs. Snavin wasn't watching, he pulled out a CD-ROM and showed it to me. It was BATTLE TANX. "I always have a copy of this with me, just in case." And he grinned.

It was Thursday, so we didn't have art or gym. After free time, we watched a social studies video about these explorers named Lewis and Clark, and it was like this long adventure story, except it was all true. The morning was going great. And the best part was I could tell the kids in my class didn't think I was the teacher's pet anymore.

But the minute I went out into the hallway to go to lunch, some kids from Mrs. Frule's class saw me and this boy said, "Hey, look! It's Jakey Drakey. Gonna eat lunch with your girlfriend Miss Cott today?"

And then three or four fifth-grade kids started saying, "Jake Drake! Jake Drake! Jake Drake!" And one of the boys knocked my lunch out of my hands, and an apple rolled out of the bag.

I wanted to start punching people, but I didn't. As I picked up my lunch and headed for the cafeteria, I thought, *Maybe things are better in my own classroom, but what about all the other kids? And all the other teachers?*

It felt like everyone else in the school was going to think I was a teacher's pet for the rest of my life.

CHAPTER NINE

CRASH LANDING, BUT SAFE

The lunchroom wasn't any better. In the milk line, a fourth grader asked me how come I wasn't cleaning tables yet. Then a fifth-grade kid said, "Hey, look! It's the original Garbage Guy!"

And when I was walking over to where Willie was sitting, a girl in Mrs. Frule's class said, "Hey, Jake— Miss Cott was talking about you in art class today. She says you are so *sweet!*" And then a whole bunch of girls started to giggle.

I sat down and tossed Willie his chocolate milk. I said, "Hi. So you think it's safe to sit with me today?"

"Yeah. I think so. Looks like you're still famous."

I nodded and bit into my peanut butter sandwich. "Yeah. Guess I'm gonna have to learn to live with it."

I leaned my head back to take a long drink of milk, but I stopped. Something was wrong with Willie, with his face. Willie looked like one of those kids in *Jurassic Park* when the Tyrannosaurus rex is trying to eat their car. I put my milk carton down and said, "What's wrong?"

And Willie whispered, "Mrs. Karp. Coming this way. Fast."

I turned around, and Willie wasn't kidding. Mrs. Karp was headed across the cafeteria. Every kid was watching her. She had this awful look on her face, and she was walking fast. And in a straight line. Toward us.

She came right up to me, and I could feel my face turn white. My heart was pounding. Mrs. Karp glared down at me. She was so tall, and it was like her face was made of stone.

Without saying a word, she reached down and took hold of my arm right above the elbow. Then real loud, she says, "You are coming to the office with me. Right now!"

Willie looked like he wanted to crawl under the table.

Then Mrs. Karp turned around and started walking. She was still holding on to my arm, and it probably looked like she was dragging me across the cafeteria. And as we walked past with everyone staring at me, in this loud voice Mrs. Karp said, "We have some things to talk about, young man. About the *ropes* in gym class. And about your *behavior* in the art room. And about something that happened Tuesday out on the *playground*." I looked up, and at one of the lunch tables, Danny Grumson was smiling at me and nodding his head. Then he put out his pointer finger and pulled it—*zip*—straight across his throat.

As Mrs. Karp pulled me across the big room, I felt myself start to blush. And I thought, *That's the last time I'll ever trust a principal. I thought I was so smart to go and talk to her. Now she's probably going to call my mom and dad, too.*

Then we were out the door, down the steps, along the front hallway, and into her office.

I hate it when I feel like I'm going to cry. Especially at school. But that's how I felt. I kept my eyes on the floor. I sat in the chair in front of Mrs. Karp's desk, and when I heard her sit in her chair, I looked up at her.

Then I looked away real quick, and then looked back again. Because I couldn't believe my eyes. Mrs. Karp was smiling. A big, warm, friendly smile.

I kept staring at her and she said, "How was that?"

I shook my head. "What? How was what?"

"My performance. How did you like my performance?" And Mrs. Karp kept on smiling. "I guess it was pretty good if it fooled you, too. Sorry, but I had to make it look real."

I shook my head, still trying to understand. "Then you're not . . . mad at me?"

She shook her head, still smiling. "No. Not at all. Remember this morning when I told you I'd think about your . . . problem? Well, I did. And what just happened, that was my solution."

And that's when I got it. It was all an act. I said, "But the ropes in gym class? I really did that."

Mrs. Karp said, "I talked with Mr. Collins, and he understands everything—and you *will* be doing more push-ups and sit-ups. Tomorrow."

"And art class?" I asked.

"Yes, Miss Cott will be making quite a big speech to you on Friday about how wrong it was to destroy school property. Which is true, of course. You shouldn't have broken that paintbrush."

Then Mrs. Karp looked at her watch. "Well, I think it's safe for you to go back and have the rest of your lunch now. But remember, Jake, this has to be our secret, or it's going to look like I've given you *special treatment*—and we wouldn't want anyone to think *that*, now, would we?"

And at that moment, if Mrs. Karp had wanted to pat me on the head, I wouldn't have minded it one bit.

So that was how the longest four days of my life finally ended. And I never told anyone about Mrs. Karp's great performance, not even Willie.

The rest of my lunch tasted great that Thursday. And I wish you could have seen the way everyone looked at me when I walked back into the cafeteria and sat down to eat.

Some kids looked at me like I was an escaped criminal. Some kids looked at me like I was a hero coming back from a war. Some kids looked at me like they were afraid to look at me. But nobody—not one kid, not one teacher, not one cafeteria lady—nobody looked at me like I had *ever* been Jake Drake, Teacher's Pet.